Mikhail Kraminsky
& other poems

AC Benus

an AC Benus Impression
San Francisco

Grateful acknowledgement is here offered
for the support and encouragement
I've received on the literary site
www.gayauthors.org.

Special thanks to Parker Owens for
checking the math of my polynomial.

ISBN 978-1-953389-15-2 (ebook)
ISBN 978-1-953389-16-9 (paperback)

MIKHAIL KRAMINSKY, AND OTHER POEMS.
Copyright © 2021 by AC Benus.

Cover photo:
Pxhere.com / detail from the Catherine Palace, representing Mikhail Kraminsky and his team's restoration work there and many other sites

Vignette:
Sourced from an 1893 American cookbook

Library of Congress Control Number: 2021915691

Table of Contents

Mikhail Kraminsky

& other poems

Poem No. 1 [1]

I live in a world
in which my words
are plucked from a limited
sea of intellect

I sit in a room while
my fate sits in another
I'm too frightened to get up and
go and look for it

Poem No. 2

    Two doors down
lies a specter of my hopes –
    they mingle
amongst his fellowship of brawn
    in open, jock-boy gropes,
never wondering why he's single

    How he came,
I can form no idea of –
    why he came,
I can only dream the same
    as above,
yet, I want to confront him by name

    Down two doors
lies a hope for my fate's way –
    I wish I knew him,

for his shyness seems not very poor
    and very near to me, so I say
I simply wish to know him [2]

Poem No. 3

I see you in a dream of blue –
the color a hazy melody –
a vision, set anew,
given me at a price hardly free.

Poem No. 4

"It is that rare thing, a perfect composition,
satisfying in its completeness, precise in its
detail – solid without weight, lightness sans
frivolity. It is like a last movement
by Mozart when the master pulls everything
together and brings off another miracle."

Poem No. 5

There was a case. In the Great Shop
    it was filled with beautiful jewels,
    also a bright red line painted down the center.

The Shop-owner said unto me
    "You may pick any of the jewels,
    as long as you pick from the left side of the case."

The jewels on the left were grand,
    each one a lovely and divine thing,
    each one purposeful and filled with subtle beauty.

The right, oh the right, had beauty unmatched,
    for every one filled my mind with joy,
    for on every face, there burned tenderness, undenied.

<u>Poem with too many names</u>

Poem No. 6

It rides on the mists of sleepy nights,
shows itself, and mysteries unbar,

Images of ghoulish fate and Elysian heights,
ambiguity unknown, buoyancy wide and far.

Such masks seem to disappear at twilight,
as sweet and calm then return,

Showing a glimpse of ponderous things out of sight,
the Universe seems as one, no ambitions, no lessons to learn.

Poem No. 7

Ship of Tyre [3]

I see a wall
its bricks make a translucent surface
clean and smooth are they
so smooth I can't see or feel their grout

I can come close
but I cannot go beyond the wall
Why? I ask myself
fingers on their surface sense them so cold

Visions betrayed
are so lovely and so very close
refined work is there
judged crudeness lives on my side of the wall

I see a wall
that I cannot break
mediocrity
I wish I've wings to fly to vast regions
        beyond
    the wall

Poem No. 8

Adventures of my Umbrella

When I was but a child,
I had an umbrella.
I was seven; it was new.

I remember it when
Seeing it the first time;
Downtown is where it was,
In some ritzy display.

In a place with glass doors,
The shop like the 'brella,
Was black – how elegant.

My mom bought two that day:
One for her; one for me.
She had had some before;
For me it was my first.

What mysteries were in
That black new umbrella;
How I longed to use it.

Then finally one day,
Rain was in the forecast;
Out of the closet it
Came for its first big use.

It wasn't easy though
To convince Mom the need
Of taking it to school.

But I argued, saying,
"Why did you buy it then,
If I can't ever use?"
She swayed; it came with me.

It didn't rain, but what
Did that matter right then,
For I'd still show it off.

Boring school, like always,
Made me long for day's end,
And "Who knows, there could still
Be a massive downpour!"

Marian looked after me
Afternoons until my mom
Could pick me up from work.

So, though a rainless day,
The school bell rang and I
Collected my things to
Trudge my way back to her.

To get to Marian's house,
I went the high-school way,
Though she told me not to.

I thought about how many
More chances I could get
To impress with my toy –
My new black umbrella.

When I walked by the grade school,
I saw the daughter of
My once-a-week tutor.

They lived in a big house
That wasn't far from mine;
My tutor was so nice,
It never seemed like homework.

My tutor's daughter asked
If I would like a ride home.
I said, "Sure, that would be nice."

I did wonder though how
She knew to take me to
My babysitter's house....
She started the right way.

She went down the right street,
But then suddenly turned
The exact opposite way.

I wanted to tell her
To go the other way –
But then, the whole idea
Seemed a very bad one.

And what of Marian?
Would she be worried when
I didn't show up soon?

So, I was on my way home;
My mind raced as to what to tell.
"Why are you home so early?"
My dad was sure to say.

These were the things I thought
As my tutor's daughter
Sped in the wrong direction.

I considered this because
My Mom hadn't given me
My very own front door key –
Wait… "I left my umbrella."

This I thought as she drove
Off with my new equipment,
But, by then, it was too late.

Now what was I to do?
I feverishly delved,
Looking for an excuse
Where my umbrella was.

Not much came right away,
Then again when asked, I
Would come up with something.

"At school," is what I said.
Mom replied, "Don't forget
About it tomorrow."
"I won't!" was my swift answer.

My brand-new umbrella
Lay on the back-seat floor:
Left but not abandoned.

I went to my tutor
Every Tuesday evening,
After dinner, from home,
I walked myself over there.

They *had* seen my umbrella!
It lay nestled against
The others in their care.

I stroked it in the hall tree,
Knowing in an hour
I'd be able to put right
A mistake that'd ballooned.

When I left, I snagged it
To take it where it would
Be finally at home.

I was out the door,
And way down the sidewalk,
When I realized I
Had a major problem.

I told my mom I had
Left it back at my school;
What could I tell her now?

What bold explanation
From my seven-year-old
Brain would explain this one –
What to do and not panic?

Starting to walk on home,
Worry marched by my side;
Suddenly I had a flash.

It wasn't a good flash,
In retrospect I know,
But despair was to blame
When I think back to it.

In my home's direction,
Near my tutor's abode,
Was a buried culvert.

I took my new shiny
Umbrella and stuck it
In the dry drainage pipe,
But felt ill doing it.

Yet, I did have a plan
To get it back next week,
Barring some rain, that is.

The week flew by slowly
Bringing Tuesday 'round to me –
It hadn't rained, so I
Hoped it was still in place.

Tutoring went quickly.
When over, I leapt out
Her front door to get it.

The path was blocked instead,
Showing me my mom with
A stranger idly talking.
My mom! What was happ'ning?

She'd never walked me home
After my tutoring.
I couldn't believe it.

After chatty intros,
To my horror, we all walked
The few blocks back to home.

I had no chance to get
My lonely umbrella;
It would have to wait longer.

The following week dragged
Slower than the previous;
It had been so long since
I'd seen my umbrella.

Back to look in the pipe,
My umbrella was gone –
I'd never see it again…

Now you see my woe,
For when I was a child,
I had an umbrella.
I was seven; it was new.

   Postlude:

Memory of love, or love of memory
I don't know which is true of my umbrella

The case now, I cannot state very calmly
Did I love then, or only hence, that umbrella

I only know if I were to run away
To the blue hills, what would occupy me there

Where the hills and my umbrella are I can't say
I only know they're gone, yet still they are there

Where are the distant, rolling blue hills of my youth?
Where do I look? To Memphis, Lincoln, or Duluth?

Poem No. 9

Lyrics:

You are a radiant sun shining on an unworthy shore
    warming sweetly regions benign
    hidden though they are in the cold dark
You stimulate them with your light.

Your light draws love from a very deep place hidden from
even me
    sweetly warming regions benign
    which I didn't realize were there
Your light, so gentle, do I need.

You are a radiant sun shining on an unworthy shore
    with your light can I take on wings
    with you can I create dreams coming true
Your thought makes words dull in contrast.

because

You *are* a radiant sun shining on an unworthy shore.

Poem No. 10

If I could burn my soul,
    all that it means to me

If my spirit were made of paper
and evil said its lines

In fire could I be born
into new life

Free from pain,
and free from strife.

Poem No. 11

AISLING

She stands upon the hill so fair,
lightness dreams for her,
Of soft, sweet, distant air,
where a wafting breeze makes her stir.

So gently she comes to moor,
as a thought in slumber does,
A heartened pang to adore,
a silent lady, forever to love.

If a tree moans, I know she nears,
her fragrance scents the air,
A perfume, subtle, familiar, and dear,
I know she comes so fair.

The Lady's calm will in me stir,
a grateful tone to bear,
For lightness dreams of her,
the Lady of the sweetened air.

Poem No. 12

She stands in misty darkness still –
　　silence is her breath
gentle motion, whitened will –
　　she of calmness does request

An effortless sea of white does fall –
　　she covers all so tenderly
a gentle scene that sings to all –
　　of peaceful, blanched tranquility

Her soul clings to the branches of trees –
　　traces still of her movement
a silent lady forever to believe –
　　sweetened white to give deludement

In darkness still does she stand –
　　colorless oblivion
her motions gentle on the land –
　　her calmness envelops all thoughts of sin.

<u>Winter Snow</u>

Poem No. 13

I have seen you everywhere
　　countless times a specterful sleep
　　the world's not real to me
　　I want to be what I can be
　　already.

The weight is smashing me
   how I long to be what I can be
   I simply face the morrow wanting
   God in Glory to fall asleep
   already.

Poem No. 14

  Haiku:

Fiery-winged fowl,
A goose of wordless feathers
Flees his woes by flight.

Poem No. 15

If God be in a bug,
we'd all better stick ourselves
under the rug.

If God be in a bug,
and he's squashed, we've all got our
burial dug.

For if you were a bug,
and had your brains smashed out by
a fool from above

You would feel a grievance done
if you were God and a bug
then squashed from above,
    so,

If God be in a bug,
we'd all better stick ourselves
under the rug.

Poem No. 16

Six $\bar{a}$ to the *zee, bee* to the *zee* minus ten *bee* to the *zee*
    minus –
Three $\bar{a}$ to the *zee, cee* to the *zee*, less five *cee* to the *zee*

Six $\bar{a}$ to the *zee, bee* to the *zee*, minus three $\bar{a}$ to the *zee,*
    cee to the *zee*
        plus –
Negative ten *bee* to the *zee* plus five *cee* to the *zee*

Three $\bar{a}$ to the *zee*, times two *bee* to the *zee* minus *cee* to
    the *zee*
        plus –
Five times negative two *bee* to the *zee* plus *cee* to the
    zee

Three $\bar{a}$ to the *zee* times two *bee* to the *zee* minus *cee* to
    the *zee*
        minus –
Five times two *bee* to the *zee* minus *cee* to the *zee*

Two *bee* to the *zee* minus *cee* to the *zee*
      times –
Three $\bar{a}$ to the *zee* minus five.

<u>Ode to a Polynomial</u>

P.S. God help me... [4]

Poem No. 17

Moonless midnight
   and memories

Phantoms in flight
   difficult to keep in solidity

Too many memories
   to remember

Such wicked abstractions
   to which I have no identity

Poem No. 18

Prelude:

I hate to be alive,
   how more simply can I say it.

I have nothing for to strive,
    no happiness in which to simply sit

What possible gifts do I have to give,
    when I take space and do nothing but stare

So I ask, for what reason do I live,
    to cease such a life, do I think to dare

My problem with that, is this,
    the world is so damn beautiful, why did God

Put a scourge like human kindness
    on the planet to muck and mess up the sod.

All I know is that:

I hate to be alive,
how more simply can I say it?

    Poem:

The blood rushing from my arms
making me impure by its super purity
rushing until perfect bliss be found.

Poem No. 19

        i.
I might have been first
Instead I am the worst

Did God make an illiterate writer
a painter with no hands

Did he make a critic for his creator
a simple fool with no fans

What exactly did God make –
a quivering mass of self-pity?

No, not God. I did that despite his sake
he is love, and cannot be flighty

ii.
The rain is coming now
How nice it would be
to be washed clean by it
but
I lack such soap.
I might have been first
Instead, I'll remain the worst.

Poem No. 20

Sweep and pound as hard as you can
    wind, throw them at me

Sweet pungent smell, clean my mind
    fury of the storm, make me see

Wetness awaken me, frighten
    me with the cold

I don't like the air I breathe now
    fill me with newly brisk air

Rain help me see me
    anew!!!

Poem No. 21

They...

...squeak, and squawk and rumble,
    and they fly.
Oh, I'd like to be an elevator humble,
    and live in the sky.

Poem No. 22

The spring is beautiful
As I watch her dress the Earth
In emotions I had almost forgot
Using colors stored in careful places
Kept safe from the frost of the soul
Safe in the warmth of knowing
That no matter what, her day will come again.

The spring is a beautiful reason
Not that she has any cause to be
Wars are still being fought
People are still hating many things.

And yet, she comes
Offering her gift to the world
No questions, no bills
She comes for reasons unknown.

With a million secret colors
She paints a million emotions
Far too many to write
And so I'm left with nothing but...

The spring is beautiful.

Poem No. 23

Each day a million thoughts are born,
each needs prove itself against reason's scorn

Wrong or right, they are our history

Filtered through the mind like sand,
they are the eternal story of Man.

Poem No. 24

She from a dream does stir
        to awaken what was forgotten
    with those gentle fingers of her –
        the land and dreams forsaken.

She in calmness does fall
      into this, our raging world of life
  till she becomes part of it all –
      the point of instinctive strife.

When she moves in her first step
      all others must dearly pay her heed
  for her birth, and her first breath –
      only then may they proceed.

She stands in airless anticipation
      bringing all to the cusp of the hour
  returning to recognition –
      for the Lady has such power.

<u>Spring Thaw</u>

Poem No. 25

Poems have dealt with life and love, and a lack thereof,
  of pretty things, and heroic man that sings

I want to think above, of what's not been thought of
  besides the same old fling, there must be something

How about some hogs, or a wagonload of logs;
  Infested with lice, or with some such device?

Puppy dogs, and little-girl frogs;
  ants, and mice – now, how do those matters entice?

Shall I ever write newly of unspoken things truly?
    after all, what's left, but burglary and theft?

Hey, now there's a thought duly, of something new and unruly
    and if I fail with heft, at least I've tried to be deft.

Oh well, with that cavort, back to mundane things of sort
    of love, of life, and songs of strife

Perhaps I'll just write of Mort, who drank a bottle of port
    and fell out of sight, from a cliff of some great height. [5]

Poem No. 26

Is there anyone happy in the world today?
    What happened to the children who used to play?
    And the preachers who used to gossip –
They don't anymore, they don't speak of it.

I know why the children don't play today;
    It's because I'm not a child's stature, per se,
    And why the preachers don't speak of it –
They haven't seen me in church for a bit.

What changes; the world or the people?
    I have, for I've lost childish glow,
    And it hurts the more I know –
Being of the earth makes me a cripple.

Poem No. 27

I look for beauty
but can find only the beast.
As children we are told to avoid it –
only purity for purities sought –
unforbidden duty
but the wrong offers such a feast
that only children can avoid it
and I am not a child with a child's thought.

coming out

Poem No. 28

Sweet embrace of a horrid thought
    a simple one, one of immense truth –
    its presence revolts me

The thought is entirely there
    though magnified by the night so still –
    the thought of who I am. [6]

Poem No. 29

You know of course I meant to go
before she went
but then she went before I got the chance to go
so now I'm going after she went
oh no.

Poem No. 30

Portrait...

My God, what a lovely face she did once possess
    filled with all the emotions we could ever need
Now is it drained of charm from every recess
    by those who claim to be her rightful seed.

All that she had, she gave; nothing is left to assess
    yet impatient fools, who only think of their greed
Try to draw blood from her every abscess
    for when she doesn't look, then her children feed.

She was young, and oh so sublime, not so long ago
    but then she bore the frightful scourge of herself
And her children, they sucked away her blooming glow
    while she raised not a finger to say no unto their pelf.

        She used to be proud
        and held her head high,
        but now covered with a shroud,
        her children ask with a sigh,
        'Is this the beauty who raised
        my sisters and brothers?
        This? Torn so by motherly duty...?'

My God, what have we done to our most important,
    life-giving mother? Please forgive our earthly sins.
We thought we would never be accountable
    and reduced to the status of your orphans.

<u>...of our Mother Earth</u>

Poem No. 31

Beauty is of itself, a whole thing.
It can't fight its enemies
And we, too stupid, don't know
What they are.
So, Beauty suffers, while
We do nothing.

Poem No. 32

In the mist, I think I can faintly see
    a vision that perhaps is of me,
but since I know myself not at all,
    in mystery it lies with my wherewithal.

Poem No. 33

Loneliness' song is slow but sweet,
    its voice, ever-constant, eternal –
Through the history of Man, its beat
    pulls us to ourselves most fraternal.

Poem No. 34

The night the poems died
    it happened all once

everything just shriveled up inside
all of it, at once.

It wasn't as painful
    as one would think
    but then, I've forgotten that pitiful
    can lead you to the brink.

I wasn't prepared to face the truth
    I'd rather lie and make believe
    and with my soul strike a truce,
    but, that I can't, I want to believe.

Malingerant coward that am I
    to hope I could cower and die
    what a sick and pain-filled lie
    because all I can do, is sigh.

Poem No. 35

I lie awake and spy
on visions of burnt dreams
flashing boldly in the empty sky
of my mind, bursting its seams…

To be anything less than a success
is to have failed totally;
not to go forward, but to regress
is to show your shame boastfully…

I've lost what I was going to say
but it doesn't matter, I'm sure,
for there'll be another day
of tortured tolerance with which to endure…

And I imagine I shall too.

Poem No. 36

I need a cure –
Does anyone know
The cure for self-contempt?

Poem No. 37

In the dreams of men
thoughts are born
specters of fame and fall
and of none at all
it merely depends on the storm
of a mind that needs a mend

Visit me tonight?
Who knows what will –
whatever it is,
whoever it is –
well, I'll remember it still
when I awake in the daylight

Should I be afraid
of phantoms unknown?
I won't wake
in the same world
I went to sleep in;
memories will have flown
and I think they haven't stayed

Then again – maybe
I'll see sweet, soothing light
that will calm and quench
my spirit's ideas there they intrench
and illuminate my sight
to enlightenment most free.

In my mind
thoughts are born
specters of fame and fall
and of none at all –
it all depends on the storm
of a mind that needs a mend

Poem No. 38

Dwight

When subtle things move behind a smile
beckoning for a chance all the while
but still unsure is he
who thinks, but wonders what could be
behind the cheerful expression that's grave
a fantasy to treasure and save

When subtle things move behind happy eyes
    that try to hide deeper things by disguise
        but leave looks to remember
        as calling cards from the lender
    visions I dare not think be true
        imaginings of immensities misconstrue

"I am very confused to meet you"
    when your eyes speak before they let you
        when your smile denotes something special
        that I can approach at the same level
    am I to act on subtle clues in scope,
        or should I stop and give up any hope?

Poem No. 39

The Materialist's Love Song

Prelude:

Sweet sound of the VCR –
    click
    rurrrrup
    and then a steady purr

From the hollow within
    come visions
    created by
    workmen unseen

I come to the VCR
when days are dark
for I know that joy is never far
from my friend who doesn't smell or bark

Happy days from the VCR –
    click
    and then a steady purr
    all this, and I never have to call it sir.

    Poem:

Things give pleasure, how can I deny?
Money gives power, as great as the sky.

    And what's the price? Oh, not much –
Well, there's no lice or stuff such –
    All you have to do, my wondering dear,
    Is give up your chance to know why we respire here.

So, you want to have? Well, have it all.
Most simply done; ignore your conscience-call,
    Life can be a daze of contentment,
So forget the maze of fulfillment.
    I say forsake all; live for the gain of money.
    What else can matter as long as the days are sunny.

    Postlude:

Pleasure marked on a physical basis
can be no more than painted faces.

Happiness doesn't lie on a dollar bill
unless it's used on the poor as a pill.
Then happiness will come to both
the Christ and the giver of hope.

Poem No. 40

Prelude:

When love's not love…
And has apathy only for hate…
When the sincerest insult is to tell the truth…

Poem:

On a summer night
When the heat is past its height
I lie awake
And wonder just what's at stake

My dream's a depressing sea
On a boat un-tethered but still not free
Sailing through a fog I cannot master
Because the mist simply rolls in faster.

I float along in the windward lee
Sensing the weight of utter despair, she,
Is a power that I won't be able to shake,
And could sink me perhaps before I wake.

Poem No. 41

Mikhail Kraminsky

Prelude:

In 1941, the City of Peter
was laid siege upon;
900 days later, it ended.
As the Nazis left
they burned the home of Peter
and his descendants, and his people.

Poem:

What monument could befit
Mikhail Kraminsky?
Not stone or brick, marble or glass –
Wood's inadequate from ages past
steel and cement aren't the clue either –
for what he has done, has made man seem bright.
Mikhail Kraminsky,
for immortality you are fit.

How can the role of hero be filled?
In you it showed simple enough.
You are the restorer of your nation's monuments,
you rebuilt what once was present,
what once was ignorantly destroyed,

but after, you saw and had no anger to display,
you only knew crying wasn't enough,
and with a hopeful sigh, sad: "We will rebuild."

In forty not-so simple years
you've built a monument to yourself
through your tireless love to restore –
from piles of rubble, towns again stand,
gilded in majesty, not remade, but reclaimed –
and you, Kraminsky, for us made it the same
palaces of others, but as a monument to yourself,
you have struck away all the tears.

The greatest triumph of Man –
you have done no less –
where others would have only anger,
you had only conviction that's stronger;
where others would fill with concrete,
you had a vision only to restore complete.
What other monument could befit a man
who has done the greatest triumph of Man
and no less?

   Postlude:

Let this be my memorial to you,
    Mikhail Kraminsky,
And please accomplish what you have to do,
Not only for Russia, but for all to know that dreams come
true,
    Mikhail Kraminsky. [7]

Poem No. 42

Sonnet:

The world calmly shouts what it has, and always will –
a question pleaded since the first wave of God's hand
with a fearlessness that's been called anything but bland –
time has not removed it; the question is posed still.
In the future people like me will get their fill? –
Doubt will come to the next, and be as sure as sand;
believe me, I see only pain from where I stand,
where so many others felt their hearts break and spill.
The question simply put: what is beauty; what is love;
Can beauty be in everything, say perhaps a foot?
Can love be in everyone, in their personal check?
The answer's seen by people who know what is above –
a joyous work of longing whose seed has taken root –
the world sings it's an unfulfilled emotional wreck.

Postlude:

What is it in the face of man
that proves he's more than simple sand?

Poem No. 43

The gentle drift of a thought
slides silently into bed
and whispers things that were said –

thoughts and wonderments of the dead,
their lives spent for what they sought.

Darkness brings the visitor
that lies besides me every night,
that brings visions of ghoulish fright –
and with the birth of day will take flight
and leave behind, less of a shell, and no victor.

<u>Night Thoughts</u>

Poem No. 44

death
    embrace me
take me away from my lover
    lonely
aggress me
    death
trees I do not need
grass I do not need
    so what's there to hold
    me
    peace I cannot find
    love I do not want
    – help us death –
    embrace me.

Poem No. 45

Qu'est-ce que l'amour?
that is the principal question
asked by some before.

I saw the door ajar
and wished I could
pry it some more –
    to inch it with purpose.

Only once was man given the sublime
and he can't see it;
thinks it's in something else.
How wrong he is.
I hope he finds the spark
of the true rhyme
that was given to us.
The one spark, that was given
    and not made.

Poem No. 46

I.
When the City of the Saint
Was the city of the West,
When all was fresh and new with paint,
This and the spring of '46 were at their best.

From the East a young man came
For an adventure to find,
Francis Parkman was his wealthy name,
And a guide is what he needed to be signed.

From the West a young man came
To the city that gave him birth,
Henri Chantillon was his name,
And a guide from the age of fifteen was his worth.

The two men came to the western city
One in search of his manhood in the West,
One for a break in his life of things pretty,
They didn't know they'd meet; they couldn't have guessed.

II.
Different men they were for sure
One a happy Easterner,
Who had never a hardship to endure,
Indians and Adventure were the West's big lure.

For the other had become
A man among his brothers,
His heart was one with the meaning of the Chisum,
His mind saw as brightly as the others. [8]

. . . .

Poem No. 47

What's the matter?
    Money again,
or shameful sin.
    What's the matter again?

Poem No. 48

We dream to become what we're not
    look for visions to be sought
        it doesn't matter if they're our own
        as long as we have them sewn
with the thread of hope in our thought.

Poem No. 49

If in days yet to come,
    no one can recall our face,
or know what we've done,
    can't fit us into a space,
can't know what we've sung
    if, they knowing we were unhappy
or know unfulfilled,
    if they know we were daffy
beyond the normal still,
    then they will find a common thread
to link them to us, at least in the head.

Poem No. 50

Like a song that wove itself into a soul
Like a glance that set into a mood
    these are abstract thoughts
    that express what I feel

Poem No. 51

You can give yourself to God
Only if you give yourself to your brothers.

Poem No. 52

You know of course I meant to go
    before she went
    but then she went before I got the chance to go
    so now I'm going after she went
Oh no.

Poem No. 53

    Prelude:

    Today I watched
the sun be born.
    In words, it went like this:

Poem:

I.

Fizz and fuzz and chill a-snap
   it's sad above the trees
Will and wile and still a-chap
   It is cold enough to freeze
Fizz and fuzz and chill a-bap
   the sun nothing more than a tease
Will and wile and still a-snap
   only a cold light edges the breeze.

II.

Hint and hue of burning blue
   an amber coal gives rise
Brace and bob of hinting hue
   through misty, drowsy skies
Rick and reel of sighing sight
   rousing thus by its color
Sent and steel of wronging right
   forgetting what was duller
Moan and moat of changing chance
   half an ellipse raises its voice
Choose and change of manly stance
   asking all to make a choice
Heat and haul of blaring new
   an amber coal gives rise
Burning off the hinting hue of blue
   ascending misty, drowsy skies.

Poem No. 54

I walk into my room the same as always
Set down my drawings too, just the same, I thought,
But I didn't know a mystery lurked for me.

Something that was changed from all the other days,
Some subtle hidden thing, something not the part,
I accidentally walked by, but didn't see.

I addressed my roommate: "How are you today?"
"Better than usual;" he's been ill you see,
Still I didn't see it. On my way I wanted to go.

Before I left though, before I could get away,
I needed a drawing; get it and I'd be free.
Bent down to get it, I saw it and said, "Oh."

A pair of black shoes. "Oh, are these yours,"
I said to my roommate. "No, I've never seen them before."
"If they're not your shoes, then why are they here, and
whose?"

I could say no more about such strange occurrences;
A pair of black shoes visits my room, what a strange scene;
Not my shoes, not his shoes, we look and wonder who?

  Postlude:

Yukio, my strange and subtle friend
    who doesn't know how to pronounce 'lend'

but can read hearts and knows what they have to send.

Poem No. 55

This is a rhyming test, so don't sound the alarm
So do not be distressed, don't sell the house and farm

   I'm simply trying a scheme, to see what I can do
   To think of something that's new, strange as that just
might seem

So to begin I will, let's see…I'll start it this way…
This is a rhyming drill, and that's all I have to say.

Poem No. 56

   In slumber days
the sky was pink with excitement
because innocency lived in a sigh.

Poem No. 57

  Prelude:

A lady does her nails, in a class about Death
   and then leaves

They're ugly red nails, in a class about Death
    they match her sleeves
Her ruddy color pales, her throat swallows a breath
    and then leaves
A lady did her nails, in a class about Death
    to match her sleeves
Turns pale and leaves.

  Poem:

There's a leaf on the floor,
All the way in the corner, under the window,
And I wonder how it got there.

Poem No. 58

  Lyric Sonnet:

What's beauty for,
if I can't embrace it?
and still the more,
to what can it befit?
why need it be,
it seems out of kilter
far beyond me,
why doesn't it filter?
So I must ask,
what can beauty be for
if in it I can't bask;

without it I can't soar?
I have one gentle task,
to know beauty once more.

   Postlude:

    To come to a dream
and not to recognize it
Is not knowing how to live

Poem No. 59

There's a stillness in my heart
    that I can't draw on this paper.

It is made of buttercups,
    or vagrants lying in the street.

How very stupid I am,
    for if I can't see it, how can you?

So, a mystery it'll remain,
    and we're better off not knowing.

Poem No. 60

I'll dream of you in the sometimes hour,
About those days of years gone past,

A haunted melody, meant not to sour,
Dried a quiet memory in a mind dyed fast.

Your eyes are set eternal in my hope,
A thing never meant to fade,
There I see you always;
What eyes can say, when words simply fade:

a cruel glance bared its bitterness,
and lasts as long as a bad Coffey dreg;
a glance if chance held the newness,
a glance of hatred lingers like the plague.

But. I'll dream of you in the sometimes hour,
About the ones I've seen in years gone past;
Some a joyous thing, others can go sour,
Dried a quiet memory in a mind dyed fast.

Poem No. 61

Prelude:

Muscle and bone, that's all it is
    blood and brains, that's all it is
        put together in a way
        that makes my humor and mind
        sing of them:

Poem:

A note of amorous kind
passed with a smiling nod

that says more than the note

she opens it like a great find
her eyes dart, a smiling nod
that says more than he wrote

gleefully she gets a pen
finds a paper that's almost blank
and jots something then

a note most amorous sent
passed with a smiling nod
that says more than the note

he opens it like a great event
his eyes dart, a smiling nod
that says more than she wrote

Poem No. 62

The King of Brooklyn

What if he were born in Brooklyn
On a morning like all the others
What if he said he was free from sin
And told us we are all brothers

What if he were born black
And said that he loved us all,
The son of us, the entire pack,
Said he'd come to teach us not to fall
 Would we listen to his call

In a public institution,
What if that is where he was born,
Would wise men kneel before his position,
    Would others decry his birth a Medicare scam

What about his very young mother,
Would we see her pain in the knowing
That her son was born to in death hover
And think him the lamb of the coming
    Would we see his calling

What if a poor child in Brooklyn
Were the King of Kings, the Prince of Peace
Would we listen to him; could we him know;
Could he fit our pre-fab image

Would he be let in the Thanksgiving Day Parade
Would our Fifth Avenue welcome him;
The bishops and shopkeepers, would they delay
The celebration till his birthday began
    Would we recognize a Christ if we saw him? [9]

Poem No. 63

A Holiday Postlude

Toe trimmings and tree trimmings
    lay together in a bag.
After Christmas, after New Year's,
    they're considered something of a nag.

What if there were a Christmas tax:
    on sack, box, and carrying crate
    on ropes, ribbons, and Scotch tape
    on bows satin, and angels in pose
    on pictures of reindeer, and on Rudolph's nose
    on Christmas tunes, and church to attend
    on tinsel gold, and cards to send
    on 'good ole times,' and many a friend
    on trees green, and carolers in white
    on sheep, and every shepherd in sight
    on wreaths holly, and berry mugs
    on mangers, and clearance sales in floods
    on jolly elves, and seasonal duds?
What if there were a Christmas tax
on the things that mean Christmas to us?

Mikhail Kraminsky, and other poems
Text Endnotes:

[1] The poems of this collection are presented sequentially from the calendar year in which I was twenty years old. That means several of the early ones (up to No. 11) were written before my birthday in February, and thus when I was still nineteen.

"I live in a world" (Poem No. 1): This is one of several in the book that might best be termed 'A voice from the closet.'

[2] "Two Doors Down": This poem was written about a mysterious and beautiful young man who occupied my old dorm room – 128 Mouton Hall – when I lived two doors down at 126. He stayed alone in the double room by choice, was tall, of medium build, had light-brown hair, and possessed an inscrutable bearing of dignity and sexiness to him. I never saw him in the cafeteria, nor had any classes with him, and barely ever exchanged more than passing greetings to him – but I remember him to this day!

[3] "Ship of Tyre": See Ezekiel, chapter 27, verse 1~36.

[4] "Ode to a Polynomial": The postscript is on the original manuscript, lol. My humble thanks to Parker Owens for checking and correcting the algebraic equation here 'poeticized.'

[5] "Poems have dealt with life": This lighthearted poem was my reaction to learning about internal rhymes and alliterations.

[6] "Sweet embrace of a horrid thought": The voice here is of one from the closet.

[7] "Mikhail Kraminsky": This poem was written after watching a documentary on television. The National Geographic Society was working with the Public Broadcasting Service to make periodic shows at this time, and one featured the ongoing work of Russian historians to restore monuments destroyed in World War II. I have looked, and not been able to find this documentary online. It has also been frustrating not finding any information on Mikhail Kraminsky when searching for him (in English, at least). I do have this mention from *The Palaces of Leningrad*, by Victor and Audrey Kennett, 1973 London. The book is ded-icated: "TO OUR BROTHER, MIKHAIL ASAREVICH KRAMIN-SKY, ARCHITECT, AND RESTORER TO HIS CITY'S MONUMENTS." So, at least I know I have spelled his name correctly.

[8] "When the City of the Saint": This is the opening fragment of an epic poem I had in mind based on the accounts from Francis Parkman's 1849 book *The Oregon Trail*. As you can see, I did not get very far.

[9] "The King of Brooklyn": Written on Thanksgiving.

Thirty-Six
early poems

Poem No. 1

Leave death alone,
for it shall take care of itself.
Concern yourself with life,
for there the sweetest pain lies.

There came upon the sea of despair
many false prophets
All proclaiming the glory of
themselves.
Believe them not, for the key
to God lies in your heart and
There alone, for God is love
and love is God, so remember
The key lies within your heart.

Poem No. 2

Haiku:

A ship sails over
the moon, gently and so free
on a sea of dreams.

Poem No. 3

Greatest Gift Given

The gift came with no bow
or in bright wrappings that tend to glow –
    Or hid in brown paper
borrowed from a good, nearby neighbor.

It came plain as can be
    sitting there for everyone to see –
Is there no sense of pride
    for this gift given for you to abide?

Or maybe, just perhaps
    this gift is not within mortal grasps –
Wide as an ocean
    I think I will call it emotion.

Poem No. 4

Winter

The winds blow themselves across barren land,
a bleak concept for summer's ban –
it is winter's triumph to be so grand.

The time is not for summer sand
nor spring's sweet fan –
now is winter, see and feel it at hand.

Poem No. 5

Prayer

Energy surrounded by many a name,
    ever changing, always the same –

Let me bask in your loving light,
    and release me from the realm of fright.

Poem No. 6

Nature softly calling
    Come, Come, Come,
To a place where She and Man are one
    Come, Come, Come,
To a place where Nature and I are one

Come

To where lions sing and birds are purring
    ...Come, Come, Come...
Nature calls to me
    ...come...come...come...
Leave life behind, come with Me and be free

come

Poem No. 7

Une Rose

How wonderful is a rose
In such soft and gentle pose

Your beauty fills the air
With color bright and fair

You fill my heart with longing
For all things grateful and belonging

A rose to man is free
Like a butterfly or a bee

I wish I could release all my earthly woes
And be like a rose

Poem No. 8

Shadows Across the Soul

The shadows on the face of the clown,
    are dark and deep, masking his smile.
The clown's rosy cheeks, so round,
    are broken, scattered for a while.

The shadows spread far and wide
    lurking in every crack of his features
Leaving no room for a sad soul to hide
    making him look like a lonesome creature.

You are such a deceitful lie,
    I tell myself the shadow can't be real,
And yet, you want to die,
    letting nothing left to feel.

Poem No. 9

Sweet darkened blanket
    in you can I find bliss

Sweet mindless oblivion
    in calm outrageousness

Unrepentant images
    painless happiness

Poem No. 10

Delusions

Sometimes when I'm alone
Just spending the day at home
I sit and dream of the day
When my children will come and say
"Papa, what was war?"

"What was it like when men would die
and mothers and children could only cry
to know that life no longer filled their lungs,
that the joy of being could no longer be sung?

"And what of hatred, Papa, do tell,
could men really fall under its spell
could men under its lure be sane
to inflict such sorrow and pain?
Papa, what of war?"

Poem No. 11

Thoughts of words

I wish I could fill the page with words to an end,
A flowing stream, through eternity to send;
Through tragedy and sin, a thought to reclaim,
A finely flowing thing forever to blame.
Words stronger than a fortress to stand against time,
Phrases so grand, so lovely, tender – forever sublime.

Poem No. 12

My face will fall
and my hair will lay
my skin just fall away
leaving bones about the hall.

It is simple fate
but men deny
that it is human to die
as certain as hate

but, if these words stand
unchanged by time and mind
a piece of me will be left behind.

Poem No. 13

Love is an emotion
that's deep as an ocean;
as violent as a flood,
and cold as mud.

Poem No. 14

Through fine crimson,
thoughts appear of sweet stillness
to flow into my mind.

Through stillness, a swath of air
    so light
calmly coming to bear
    itself by night
breaks my thoughts of sweet
    oblivion

Poem No. 15

La vie

I step alone into the dark
fearful of what seems so stark

Alone we all must enter
today or tomorrow, it all finds center

If only it wasn't so dark
and hopelessly bleak from the start

Then hope would be given a chance to live
and I, perhaps, a chance to give.

Poem No. 16

Suicide

The darkened word, the terrible thought
    it haunts me now to be sought
Such pain it holds, how upset am I
    for what strange comfort seems by its side
The darkened thought, the terrible word
it visits me now; how strangely absurd.

Poem No. 17

Through a sullen window
    a thought born of darkness' glow

Has seen a million nameless hours
    felt nothing for the countless souls it sours

Stillness creeps in the night
    and falls into dust with the light

How many thoughts born in the dark
are progeny of stillness, bearing her birthmark?

Poem No. 18

    The plateau of man's dreams
is reached first by the heart,
next by the mind,
then by the hands,
and finally, by his feet.
It's a long hard haul from
A man's dreams to the place
where he ultimately stands.

Poem No. 19

To judge something as an individual
is to ignore its potential as a whole.

Poem No. 20

Sweet surrender of a lunar teardrop,
falling softly, ever softly to Earth,
towards the remnants of its happiness.
Plop. Ripple, ripple. Then
gone with none the wiser.

Poem with No Name

Poem No. 21

Through fine crimson thoughts
    an air of sweet stillness
    flows into my mind

Through quietude, a shudder of air
    so light
calmly comes to me to bare
    itself by night

Breaking my thoughts of sweet
    oblivion

Poem No. 22

Only things of confidence tend to stay;
the brash and new fade to yesterday.
The merit of character needs be grand
for it through eternity to stand.

Poem No. 23

The world shrinks with my every heartless thought –
Soon I feel I will be alone
Standing in a knot.

Poem No. 24

"Romance"

The night is for "Romance"
Calm and sure in its stance
Forever to live in the night
Unimagined by human sight
The night remains for "Romance"

How can the mind comprehend
Phrases so lovely to bring hate to an end
The night is for romance's glow –
The maestro lives for all who know

Poem No. 25

10 minutes to eat
4 hours to sleep

3 years to go

<u>My School Life</u>

Poem No. 26

Ashes

I looked down into my tea
And what do you think I happened to see?
Ashes, ashes in my tea.
They sit, they bob, they float and stare
They prance about and put on airs
Those ashes
Ashes in my tea.
The renewal of life, the hatred of death
Everyone sighs in deep regret
Except those ashes
Ashes in my tea.

Poem No. 27

I sloshed through the slush looking for a *Raison* –
A perfectly plum, sweet, *Raison*…
Smooth and tender, to warm against the cold
I struggle through, seeking the Raison of gold.

Poem No. 28

I wish I could fall into a sleep so deep
As to relinquish life's belief –
For mediocrity haunts me so.

I into a gentle spiral fall
Downward, as a leaf to Autumn's call –
Like my heartbeat, methodically slow.

Poem No. 29

The hypocrites' mandatory cry
I don't know which is worse
the use of God's name being perversed
or fools, their soul to buy

The stamping of people in need
their only sin, being who they are
a mark to wear like a Nazi star
too tragic to think, yet we must heed

Soviet tanks poised in our mind
ready to destroy at any wince
with missiles there to convey the hints
    that men be free wherever one's to find

    Men destroying other men
for the name of a piece of land
which is as futile as a bound hand
    only through life with each other do we understand

    that this is not a game
or a huge cheap circus
it is our chance to give purpose
    to who shall never see peace the same

    Today I watched the evening news
to see what things were done
on Earth by people with guns
    March 24th, 1987, how things fused.

Poem No. 30

    What is it about the night?
   Of its solidly abstract flavor
    How can it hold me so

What is it about the night?

    And what of the moon's flight?
   Thrust like a new-born child
    Cold and naked, humble and low

What is it about the night?

The sea of gloom that steals the light
And the hope of dreams with it
Help me, God; my mind wants to know

What is it about the night?

<u>Goldberg Variations
in the Night</u>

Poem No. 31

What subtle fare
can be called a pear

Skin translucently light
flesh, yellow sweet and bright

Shiny sleek appearance do
a succulence lively new

Ode to a pear glossy and fair
what a glorious thing you are;
you creation of God, you known as a pear

<u>Ode to a Pear</u>

Poem No. 32

I saw two Christs on the street today
one was hungry, the other didn't say

On the big street they stand
mother with child in hand

No father to see
but it's not a fashion a father to be

"Something for the baby," one Christ called out
the voice was pitiful, without a doubt

It was pity I lacked, so with eyes bowed
I walked along, amidst my fellow crowd

It's a terrible thing we do to ourselves
this impulse to put other people on shelves

I saw two Christs on the street today
one was hungry, the other didn't say.

But I walked by them and went on my way.

<u>Soul of Mine</u> [1]

Poem No. 33

We enter this world naked and alone
and are expected to leave it
Clothed and befriended.

We come into the world naked and screaming
and are expected to leave it
    Clothed and silently.

Naked and alone
    naked and screaming
Clothed and befriended
    clothed and silently
Is that all life can be reduced to?

    <u>Super Inn Heaven</u> [2]

Poem No. 34

How do you inspire tea-flavored water –
How do you make it know the power of knowledge?

In a sense, it's meaningless slaughter
    not to inspire tea-flavored water.

Poem No. 35

Ode to Hate

I hate hope
    it's for the birds
I hate hope
    in other words
Pass the rope.

Hope nullifies the mind
    to love every new day
Which makes all very blind
    to the pain that is April through May.
Look, there's no hope to find.

I hate hope
    it's for the birds
I hate hope
    in other words
Call the Pope.

Poem No. 36

Of sweetened gloom that wraps the trees,
Changing their cloak to fiery leaves,
Coldness plants his death-bearing seeds,
Which cling to life for his Mother's needs.

Sweet surrender of death, un-flowered,
That life's fiery spring hath sown,
His greatest fear to be left alone,
Thrust is he into the great unknown.

Of tremendous injustice done,
To one, to him, to all, to none,
To move for the new that has begun,
For all need the warmth of the newborn sun.

<u>The new word</u> [3]

Thirty-Six Early Poems
Text Endnotes:

[1] "Soul of Mine": This was inspired by an incident on Michigan Avenue in Chicago. One of our instructors in the Fine Arts Department, Rodney Winfield, organized quarterly trips for students to spend a weekend in Chicago and see the latest show at the Art Institute. (We attended the one on John Singer Sargent.) I went out that Friday night to walk to the Rookery and Sears Tower. On the way, I overheard two sailors being propositioned for a $10 –round of oral sex by a thin woman; they declined. Soon after, I saw the pair mentioned in this poem.

Incidentally, there is a slightly revised version of this poem dated "Oct. 22nd 1990 – 2 days after." I believe this is a reference to two days after having slept with my first man, Richard, an English professor at the University of Missouri Saint Louis (UMSL). I remember sending him a few of my poems, and this one specifically. About it, I told him the form and polish may be rough, but in my opinion I could not come up with a more impactful concept. He did not reply.

[2] "Super Inn Heaven": The title is a sardonic reference to the heavenly nightclub in the concluding scene of the 1983 Monty Python film *The Meaning of Life*.

www.ingramcontent.com/pod-product-compliance
Lightning Source LLC
Chambersburg PA
CBHW071314200626
46813CB00015B/2203